THE
SEVENTH
RAVEN

THE
SEVENTH
RAVEN

By **DAVID ELLIOTT**

Illustrations by **ROVINA CAI**

HOUGHTON MIFFLIN HARCOURT

BOSTON NEW YORK

hmhbooks.com

The text was set in Aldus LT Std.
Cover design by Sharismar Rodriguez
Interior design by Sharismar Rodriguez

The Library of Congress Cataloging-in-Publication data is on file.
ISBN: 978-0-358-25211-5

Manufactured in the United States of America
DOC 10 9 8 7 6 5 4 3 2 1
4500819096

To my COVID companions:
Hester, Jane, Kyoko, Pam, Sinan.
I'm with Proust:
"Let us be grateful to the people
who make us happy."

*The privilege of a lifetime is
to become who you truly are.*

—Carl Jung

1

CHANGE

AND this is the forest
With its primeval trees
And their taciturn trunks
And their hungering roots
Like curious tongues
That kiss the hard stones
And lap the warm rain
And speak to the earth
In the language of trees

And here are the limbs
Their itinerant twigs
The finely veined leaves
That are unblinking eyes
And the eyes watch the wolf
And the eyes watch the bear
And the eyes watch the back
Of the ravening boar
That runs wild through the forest
And when the wind howls
The eyes tumble down
And leave the trees blind

Behold the rough bark
With its numberless ears
That cling to the tree
And hear the birth pangs
Of the fox and the deer
And the growl of the cat
And the break of the branch
And the flight of the stag
And the screech of the owl
And the flap of its wing
And the cry of the hare
And the rip of soft flesh
And the silence of blood

AND this is the river
That runs through the forest
And the river's a rope
That cannot be tied
And the river's a secret
That cannot be told
And the river's a riddle
That cannot be guessed
And the river's a snake
Ever shedding its skin
And the river's a bow
On the strings of the earth
And the river's a mouth
That devours the sun
And the river's a throat
That swallows the moon
And the river's a song
That sings to itself
In the ancient and sibilant
Language of rivers

AND this is the cottage
That's built near the river
Its timbers are aching
Its floorboards are cracking
And creaking they're quaking
From so many boots
Stomping in stamping out
Eight pairs of boots
Stomping in stamping out
So many boots
Stomping in stamping out
Day after day after day after day
And the hearth burns too hot
And the thatch whispers *Stop*
And the footsteps are heavy
And the joists beg for mercy
But the heels have no pity
And the boots they keep coming
Eight pairs of boots
Stomping in stamping out
Day after day after day after day

AND here are the boys
Who live in the cottage
The eldest is Jack
And the next one is Jack
And the third one's called Jack
And the fourth's known as Jack
And the fifth says he's Jack
And they call the sixth Jack
But the seventh's not Jack
The seventh is Robyn
And this is his story

ROBYN

They called me Robyn. How did they know from
    the very start
that the murmuring beat of my infant heart
would not conform to the rhythms of my brothers'?
One no different from the other,
and insensible to the smart

sting of thorns on the rocky ground. Each of us,
    it seems, has his part
to play; theirs is earthbound, like our father's,
    their feet planted in the dirt.
But I love the sky, its incandescence, its infinity,
    its colors.
And they called me Robyn.

The naming of children is a fine and subtle art.
Parents must consider everything the name imparts.
Was it merely accident or the instinct of a mother
that mine hints at altitude and air, flight and feather?
Whether luck or Fate—Fortune's sly, unyielding
    counterpart—
they called me Robyn.

ʌND here is the man
Who lives in the cottage
That's built near the river
That runs through the forest
He calls himself Jack

And here is Jack's axe
With its bright-sharpened tongue
And its bright-sharpened will
And its head-banging anger
Its terrible temper
Its loathing of rest

And this is Jack's saw
With its sharp crooked teeth
And its lunatic grin
And its sickening song
And insatiable greed
And its obsessive need

To go forth
and come back
        To go forth
and come back
        To go forth
and come back
        To go forth
and come back

AND day after day after day after day
Jack swings the sharp axe
And pulls the sharp saw
And curls the tongues
And tramples the eyes
And deafens the ears
And brings the trees down
He wants to know why
He has seven sons
When night after night after night after night
He falls on his knees
And clasps the scarred hands
That hold the dark beads
And bows the big head
That holds the dark eyes
And shuts out the noise
Of his sons in their sleep

And prays for a daughter

JACK

I do not ask for much or often,
but give me a daughter to soften
the keenly tapered edge of our lives.
Like an assassin, each day arrives,
shining, silent with his best-loved knives,
impatient to cut us down, impale,
overpower us as we travail.
It's the blighted fate of men like me
to wrestle with the despondency
yoked to their crippling poverty.
I need to hear a daughter's laughter,
see a daughter's gentle smile after
a long day's labor with seven boys—
the sweating, the hunger, and the noise.
Grant me the tender pleasures, the joys
that only a daughter can impart
to a father's troubled, loving heart.
Do this and I'll never ask again.
Amen. Amen. Amen. And amen.

AND this is Jack's wife
Let's call her Jane
Jane is a marshal
Her hands are her armies
Her fingers the soldiers
That follow Jane's orders
To break the hard earth
And plant the hard seeds
And pull the sharp weeds
And bake the coarse bread
And spin the fine thread
And weave the rough cloth
And mend the torn smocks
And the eight pairs of socks
Of her husband and sons

And when the night comes
And her husband is sleeping
And the Seven are sleeping
And the red cow is sleeping
And the horned goat is sleeping
And the fat hen is sleeping
And the kitten is sleeping

And all the world's sleeping
Jane lies awake

And dreams of a daughter

JANE

My boys and their father, they work hard
bringing down the trees, hands bruised and scarred
when a knot may cause the saw to slip.
But at least they have companionship.
There are days that loneliness will grip
and knead me, as if I were but dough.
But if I had a daughter, then . . . oh,
a girl to talk to! Someone like me,
a girl to ease the monotony
of this thrusting masculinity
that each day I am a witness to—
the constant fights to determine who
is strongest, their manners rude and coarse.
I could admonish them till I'm hoarse,
but they're men, and strangers to remorse.
I love my boys, but I cannot breathe.
Beneath this bridled calm, I seethe.
Some days I wish I could disappear.
I need a girl, a daughter with me here.

AND there's hair in the milk
And a smell in the cheese
And a snake in Jack's boot
And worms in the fruit
And a hole in Jane's pail
And the rye starts to fail
Mold grows on the bread
And the kitten is dead
And there's spot on the wheat
And rot in the goat
And bloat in the cow
And the thatch has turned black
And the axe bounces back
There are too many Jacks
There are too many Jacks
There are too many Jacks
There are too many Jacks

ROBYN

There are many days I wonder—why me?
Why was I born into this family?
This body? This time? This land? This space?
Did nature play a joke or simply misplace
the instructions about who I was meant to be?

I am different from them. It's not hard to see
the disappointment in my father's face—
part bewilderment, part disgrace.
And there are many days

I wonder why both my future and my history
feel so much like a mockery.
Am I expected to erase
every longing, every dream, every trace
of who I am, keep hidden everything I know is *me?*
There are many days I wonder.

BUT the planets spin round
And night tumbles down
And Jack says to Jane
Let us lie close
And let us unbind
All our fear and our sadness
Our worry and trouble
And Jane says to Jack
Come and lie close
And let us unbind
All our fear and our sadness
Our worry and trouble
And when it is done
The night lifts and leaves
A light in the room

And a girl in Jane's womb

AND the cow's milk is sweet
And the goat starts to bleat
And the hen lays her eggs
The dough sighs in relief
And the axe tells a joke
And the saw is relaxed
And the forest is singing
And the wild boar's singing
And the Jacks all are singing
And all the world's singing

ROBYN

And I sang too, just like the rest.
Louder even, higher, lest
they discover the secret I was hiding.
Yes, my sister's birth would bring us an inciting
joy. But joy is a capricious guest,

a mistress of the brutal jest.
For just as night is pressed
against the clear light of day, I saw an unnatural
    thing bearing
down upon the empty cradle, waiting.
But I sang too,

though my heart was throbbing in my chest.
The shadow lingered, its intention veiled, unguessed,
yet how sharply I thought I felt its sour and
    future sting.
Eyeless, it watched me, silent, smirking
like a snake that finds its way to the woodlark's nest.
Yet I sang too.

AND the bones grow and harden
And Jane is a garden
And the abdomen swells
And Jane is a bell
And the fingers can curl
And Jane is a world
When she takes to her bed
But high overhead
The thunder complains
And it rains and it rains and it rains and it rains
And the baby won't come
And it rains and it rains
Day after day
It rains and it rains
And still it won't come
And it rains and it rains
Jane cries in her pain
Night after night after night after night

ᴀɴᴅ the river's a serpent
That swallows the land
And the wind is a serpent
That writhes in the air
And the lightning's a serpent
That strikes at the trees

The Jacks fall to their knees
And the earth leaps and bounds
And the thunder resounds
And the sky is a shroud
And the boar's squeal is loud
And the day turns to night
And the moon gives no light
And the wolves whine and cower
And the morning is sour
And the thatch it is bleeding
And hope is receding
And the trembling world's pleading
But when all is forsaken
And when all is forlorn

The baby is born

AND this is the baby
Who lies in the cradle
That rocks in the cottage
That's built near the river
That runs through the forest
And the baby's a fish
Whose gills will not pump
And the baby's a locust
Whose back will not sing
And the baby's a seed
Whose roots will not push
And her arms will not flex
And her hands will not grasp
And her color is gray
And her heartbeat is slow
And her eyes are closed tight
And she's silent as prayer
And gasping for air
And the axe wants to cry
And the thatch wants to cry
And the wild boar's crying
And Jane she is crying
And Jack he is crying

And the Jacks they are crying
And Robyn is crying
But the baby's not crying

The baby is dying

JACK

So this is Your answer to my prayer?
Not joy or solace but bleak despair
when I have done everything I can
to be a dutiful, honest man?
This is Your blessing? Your so-called plan?
To give my daughter life but not breath?
To honor her birth and mourn her death
all in the course of a single day
is how You have chosen to repay
my virtue and devotion? You say
we mortals can never understand
Your mysterious ways. In Your grand
and sacred scheme, all will be revealed.
Our pain comforted. Our grief repealed.
Our sins forgiven. Our sorrow healed.
And You ask me to believe it's true.
You demand that I have faith in You.
You and Your sanctimonious jokes.
You are nothing but a cruel hoax!

JANE

No one can feel more heartache than I.
I gave her life. Must I watch her die
helpless, suffering, gasping for air?
My daughter! It's more than I can bear,
an anguish that mothers everywhere
fear—this dead and stiffening sorrow.
Tomorrow and tomorrow and tomorrow and tomorrow,
each hour of the raw future defiled,
each empty minute unreconciled
to the presence of an absent child
whose blood and heartbeat are all my own.
Her flesh is my flesh! Her bone, my bone!
Every endless, lifeless hour the same.
Every mote of dust whispering her name.
It's a feral grief I cannot tame.
But his pain is from a different page,
its columns filled with blasphemous rage,
an imprudent and destructive thing.
I fear for what the future may bring.

ROBYN

Everyone thinks it should be me.
Everyone knows. Everyone can see:
What's happening isn't just or fair.
How is it that she struggles for air,
suffering from some unnamed malady,

while he, so wrong, an anomaly,
breathes with such impunity? How can that be
when she, so right, is suffering there?
Everyone thinks it should be me

who fades from life and memory.
They shake their heads; they all agree.
Me for whom they say a prayer.
Me whose bones lay white and bare
throughout vacant eternity.
Everyone thinks it. It should be me.

AND here is the priest
With his Latin and linen
His cincture and tonsure
His alb and his incense
His prayers and his penance
His sign of the cross
And his story of loss

And the axe bows its head
And the saw shuts its mouth
And the thatch genuflects
And the wild boar kneels
And the hallowed trees kneel
And Jack and Jane kneel
And all the Jacks kneel
And Robyn too kneels

But the priest doesn't kneel
The priest stamps his heel
He cannot repeat
The abracadabra
He cannot perform
His arcane ministrations

He cannot baptize
Jack and Jane's daughter

Until he has water

AND Jack cries to his sons
Run to the river
And fetch the priest water
He will not provide
For your sister's long journey
Without its deep magic
And do not delay
For time is a river
A dissolute lover
Caressing the boulders
Until they are pebbles
That sink to the bottom
And chant the death rattle
For what they once were
And what might have been

JACK says to his brothers
I am the eldest
So I'll fetch the water
For that is my privilege
My duty and honor
The pride of my birthright
My charge and commission
So it has been
And so it will be

Tradition is prison
Says next-in-line Jack
So I'll fetch the water
For I am the fastest
Lean and most nimble
I'll bring the priest water
Before you begin
And Father will know
That I am a man

But I am the planet
The next Jack announces
Whose orbit he spins to
The breath of his laughter

The blood of his soul
So I'll fetch the water
To prove that I love him

The fourth Jack is silent
He frowns and conspires
I'll fetch the water
While these blockheads argue
Then Father will see
That I am his favorite

The fifth Jack declares
That he'll fetch the water
He's not sure he means it
He fears the deep river
Its buried ambitions
Its chilly affections
Its unnatural talents
And interrogations

Let me fetch the water
The last Jack announces
For I love our sister
And closely remember

The dark salty ocean
Where last she floated
Before the great flood
That carried her here
To die in her cradle
A fish without water
Washed up on the strand
Of this earthly sphere

ROBYN

But it is I who grab the dinted pail.
I run as if it is the Holy Grail
to the waiting river's edge and dip it in.
But then I hear the jealous din—
my brothers. Like a destructive gale

they descend while our frail
infant sister, choking and pale,
lies in her cradle, dying and thin.
It is I who grab the dinted pail

and I who let it go. I who cannot prevail.
I who fumble, quail,
and watch the bucket drop and spin
beneath the river's thirsty skin.
I try to save my sister, try, but fail.
It is I who grab the dinted pail.

JACK stares at his sons
With loathing and rancor
Each one is a fool
A blister a canker
And Robyn's a weakling
Girlish and slender
Too light on his feet
Too feeling too tender
And the others are brutes
Uncouth and unthinking
Jack sees the pail sinking
And beyond retrieving
And his daughter is dying
And the thatch it is crying
And the axe it is grieving
And Jane beyond reaching
And beyond retrieving
She's sobbing and wailing
Imploring beseeching
She falls to the ground
Convulsing and keening
And the priest shakes his head

And the girl is near dead
And the universe shrugs
Without sense without meaning

ΛND Anger's a beetle
That feasts on the soul
And Sorrow its grub
They swallow Jack whole
He raises his arms
And cries to the heavens
Why have You cursed us
With son after son
When we have begged You
To give us a daughter
What have we done
That You have so plagued us
Why must they live
While she lies here dying
Our daughter our prize
Our one consolation
These boys are a torment
No better than ravens
Eaters of carrion
Scourge of the sky

He utters these words
And seven new birds
Appear overhead
Not there before

And the boys are no more

AND six fly together
A maelstrom of beak
And talon and feather
And the sky it is bruised
With the beat of their wings
And the air it is pierced
With the clack of their beaks
And the rasp of their *kra-a-a-a*
And the croak and the screech
Of the anguish of flight

Where are the legs
To carry us home
Where are the backs
To help us stand straight
Where is the skin
To bring us our pleasure
Who is our father
Where shall we go
What is our mother
How can we know
Where to sleep
What to eat
How to live
Where to fly
And when the end comes
Who will pray for our souls
As they drift through the void
Of the unfeeling sky

BUT one flies alone
In the luminous space
His wings are a wonder
Of genius and grace
He wheels in bright silence
He does not complain
He soars in the gap
Between pleasure and pain
And wonders at nature's
Cosmic mistake
His father's invective
Alive in his smallness
The change in perspective
The bones that are hollow
The back that is feathered
He dips like a swallow
No longer tethered
No longer bound
By his feet on the earth
By a home on the ground

ROBYN

what   I   agony bones

happened   legs

dying   pain   intensifying   cannot see

my hands   my arms   atrophy

brothers crying

frightened   dying

body now solidifying   how can this   be

has gravity abandoned

me

JACK watches the ravens
Circle and spiral
Higher and higher
Smaller and smaller
The shrill strident choir
Diminishing fading
Until there is only
The squalor of silence
And the heavens are empty
And the forest is empty
And the wild boar's empty
And the horned goat is empty
And the fat hen is empty
And the red cow is empty
And Jack he is empty
And Jane she is empty
And the cottage is empty

BUT the cradle's not empty
Therein lies the baby
Jack and Jane's daughter
Their treasure their prize
Their one consolation
Her brothers now vanished
A strange delegation
To all things that fly

JANE runs to the cradle
And falls to her knees
She cannot take in
What she hears
What she sees
The baby is breathing
And pink as a rose
The baby is cooing
She wiggles her toes
Her arms they are dancing
Her legs are conducting
Her lungs they are pumping
Her heart is thump-thumping

Jane watches her daughter
Take in the sweet air
The cottage rejoices
The saw says a prayer
The priest disappears
He is no longer needed
Jack and Jane's plea
Has not gone unheeded

The sons have departed
A daughter emerged
A new life has started
As others were purged

THE arms of the balance
Eternally shifting
For some they are falling

For others they're lifting

ROBYN

earth far below

the wind   sighing

are these   wings?   Can

I be flying?

What is   this   dream? I dare

not   guess.   I think it might be   happiness.

DISCOVERY

IN the deep river
Days settle and drown
They surrender in silence
As they go down
Months caught in whirlpools
Break up on the rocks
Years drift away
Past shipyards and docks
Like all rusted trappings
Of humanity
Pale and exhausted
They dissolve in the sea
And re-form as coral
Starfish baleen
The river is surging

The girl is fifteen

APRIL

My mother always says they named me April
because I was like spring—a new beginning.
They were unhappy, alone, she said, until
the day I came into their lives, stuck, spinning
like the wooden tops that Father made
when I was just a girl in braids.
But is that really true? I often wonder
if there is something hidden under
their fond attention, their sweet and loving words.
I can't explain . . . I wish I could say why,
but lately when I look up at the sky,
and especially when I watch the patterns made
    by circling birds,
  I am struck with the unquiet feeling
    that there's something they're not saying,
      something they're concealing.

JANE

I will not let my daughter suffer.
It's my duty to act as the buffer—
like a shield against a driving rain—
between my girl and needless pain.
A mother's contract is to maintain
her balance, ignore what she's feeling.
There are times I find myself reeling
at the loss of my beautiful boys.
But every clever woman employs
tricks to silence the terrible noise
that's exploding daily in her head.
So, at night, when I lie in my bed
I say their names again and again,
denouncing that obscene moment when
my husband's rage banished my young men.
She will never learn about that day,
which is the reason I say
that if I lie, it must be understood!
I do it only for her own good.

APRIL

I've asked about this brooding mystery.
I want to know what they are hiding;
the secret that they keep from me
hangs like an invisible veil dividing
us. I can see deception in their eyes.
But they insist it's otherwise
and say it's only my imagination.
And yet this powerful sensation
will neither fade nor depart.
It's there especially with my father.
I know there's something bothering
him, some bitter pain locked deep within his heart.
    And the thing that gives me greatest pause?
    The awful fear that I'm the cause.

JACK

I can never tell her what occurred.
I was angry and each angry word—
a wolf bursting from its musky den.
I am no different from many men;
I have a man's red temper, and when
it sometimes gets the better of me,
any fair-minded person can see
I am not the one who is at fault.
Anger is a force you dare not halt.
Think of the hot-blooded stag that vaults
from the brush: Stop it at your peril.
Passion's natural; nature's feral.
I miss my sons, their bawdy, roughneck ways.
But time heals all, so everyone says,
and my sorrow is offset by days
with my daughter. She must never know
what happened those many years ago.
Why burden her with that history?
If she knows, she might blame me.

SHE works in the dairy
The cows make obeisance
The air smells of jasmine
The milk tastes of honey
She walks in the fields
The earth shields her footsteps
From all its sharp edges
The snakes and the wasps
Renounce their grim venoms
She sits in the garden
The stones shed their anger
The bees sing like thrushes
The worms stave their hunger
The centipede sleeps
But forces unseen
Are shaping her future
And no one can guess
The secrets they keep

APRIL

In spite of my suspicions, my life here is good.
Still, I do sometimes feel lonely.
The day is filled with chores, hauling wood.
But like so many other only
children, I have found a way to keep
my own company. Each night, before prayers and sleep,
I play a clarsach harp that Father carved for me
from the bole of an ancient hornbeam tree.
My parents say I have unusual talent,
that my music is beyond compare,
but I know that parents everywhere
say things to help their children feel content.
   Still, when I play the harp and sing,
   I feel as if my soul has sprouted wings.

AND this is the harp
With its bittersweet strings
And its arms carved with wings
That were meant to be angels
But the wood of the hornbeam
Knew the truth of Jack's heart
It would not surrender
Its grain to his art
It guided his chisel
It flouted his will
Leading his gouge
Not stopping until
The cherubs and seraphs
That Jack had intended
Morphed and amended
Themselves into ravens
Six on the frame
Three on each side
Each beak startled open
Open to chide
Their affrighted creator
Who looked on in wonder
His awe even greater
When he saw what appeared

On the harp's gleaming sound box
Which he had veneered
With the wood of the birch
A magnificent raven
Aloft on its perch
The carving so skillful
That no human hand
Was behind such perfection
He'd thought to carve angels
Life made a correction

Jack stared at the image
With fear and dismay
Truth is relentless
Truth finds a way

Λnd deep in the forest
Six ravens are feeding
Their bird hearts are beating
Their talons are kneading
The earth as they cry

Once we were men
With fists big as boulders
And voices like thunder
We set back our shoulders
And carried our burdens
Proud of our vigor
Our hair thick as forests
That grow on the mountain
Our skin clear as August
Our eyes fine and bright
As the calendar's stars
Our father betrayed us
We thought that he loved us
Instead he has damned us
To eternal shame
Now we are scavengers
Death's angry stewards
Dressed always in mourning
Debased and dejected
Without home or name

We're not like our brother
We can't understand him

He does not complain
For all that we've lost
Our manhood our futures
Discarded and tossed
On Time's rotting midden
But he does not sorrow
Although our hearts break
He was always a stranger
Distant opaque

ROBYN

I hear my brothers' bitter grief—their plans,
      their dreams, their young and lusty time all
stolen from them, but without a thief to
      prosecute and hang for this alleged
crime. The searing pain impossible to
      bear. The biting excavation of each
bone. And now they find thick talons where there
      once stood brawny legs. They bemoan the
shallow, rapid breath, and fear the naked,
      raw confusion to be one kind of thing
then suddenly another. They find a
      feathered, dazed illusion where once their eyes
beheld a loving brother. Forsaken
      and misfigured, they feel unfairly cursed.
They cannot see the irony: Our fates
      have been reversed. How strange it is that they
now feel so out of place and wrong, while I
      in soul and body know I finally
belong. As for our reckless father, when
      it comes to me, how can I be
resentful? His anger set me free.

AND these are the hands
Of Jack and Jane's daughter
The same hands that help
Her mother and father
The same hands that milk
The red cow each morning
The same hands that churn
The cream into butter
The same hands that carry
The wood for the fire
She touches the harp
Her fingers are rivers
Graceful and flowing
Her thumb is a deer
Alive in the clearing
Her muscles are birdsong
Supple and daring
Drawing strange tunings
Hypnotic and fairy
The melodies soaring
The resonance clear
And the thatch finds its meaning

And the young field is greening
And the wild boar's leaning
Closer to hear

APRIL

Many days, as I go about my chores
my idle mind wanders where it chooses.
It carries me to foreign lands and far-off shores
and helps to pass the time, diverts me and amuses
when restlessness becomes an enemy.
Often, strange impressions come to me,
but one, especially, leaves a residue
of shining truth, and yet it can't be true.
I am taken by the silly, childish notion
that the harp and I share a common fate.
What that might be I can't anticipate,
but it fills me with such deep and powerful emotion
    that each day I hold the harp more dear,
    and always want it next to me. I am uncalm
        when it's not near.

BUT the harp cannot mute
The oracular voice
That speaks to her nightly
No rest and no choice

APRIL

Seven. Seven acorns on the ground.
That is how the dream begins.
Seven. Like the deadly sins.
I look at them, then turn around.
But something makes me look again,
and in their place stand seven men.
Six of them look back at me,
in their eyes, an earnest plea.
But the seventh turns his back.
He will not let me see his face;
silent, steadfast in his place,
he turns a pure and shining black
   and rises slowly in the air
    to leave me, weeping, standing there.

JANE

It's true that nothing lasts forever.
April's not a fool. She's too clever
for the lie to survive much longer.
Every night her dreams get stronger,
destroying her peace, prolonging her
doubts. I hear her cry out in her sleep
and wonder how much longer I can keep
up with this cruel hypocrisy.
My husband, Jack, says, *Wait and see—*
she'll soon be fine. We don't agree.
I know the time has come to tell her,
but I'm afraid it might compel her
to behave foolishly or rash.
She's young, and the young are often brash.
How quickly fire becomes ash
when what is safe gainsays what is right.
The night is day and the day is night.
I love my daughter—but all's askew.
I no longer know what I should do.

JACK

Things are perfect just the way they are.
No point in taking this too far—
these fantastic, silly dreams, I mean.
For girls this age, dreams are routine,
which is why I am not at all keen
on saying more than necessary.
This whole business is temporary.
It's foolish to anticipate regret.
Nothing bad has happened yet.
But Jane's a woman, and women fret.
She says our daughter is acting strange.
I have to admit there's been a change
in her optimistic temperament.
I can see she's worried, less content.
But is that a reason to invent
some fantasy about what she knows?
Girls are moody; that's how it goes.
There's too much drama, too many tears.
Oh, how I wish my boys were here.

WHAT once he cursed
He wishes for
He cannot change
What came before
There are no boys
He has no sons
What's said is said
What's done is done

But each night
In their rookery
In a mountain
Made of glass
Six brawling ravens
Roost together
Foul of mood
And foul of feather
Ill-tempered bitter
Sour glum
They hate the woods
That once they loved
They hate what they've
Become

BUT a seventh
Roosts alone
In the mountain
Made of glass
His beak a shining
Onyx moon
His eyes two onyx stars
He thinks about
What's come to pass
A midnight avatar

ROBYN

Each evening when the setting sun retires,
    we find ourselves drawn here to sleep and rest.
An inner voice cajoles and then conspires
    to bring us to this glazed, uncommon crest,
a mountain made of glass, its brittle peak
    sequestered in the clouds. My brothers, in
jarring voices shrill and loud, say it's all
    part of the curse. They petition every
day for the spell to be reversed, and hope
    a mighty wizard's wand will wave and set
them free. That's not the case with me. I am
    altogether reconciled to
existence in the wild. Yet I cannot
    help but ask why we spend our nights
in this stifling place instead of sleeping in
    the wildwood, beneath the winking stars.
This mountain is a crystal cell without
    guards or iron bars. We are unnaturally
protected, transparently preserved.
    But for what I cannot guess. I am
uneasy and unnerved.

AND inside the cottage
April is dreaming
The axe it is steaming
The thatch it is screaming
The horned goat is foaming
The saw has gone roaming
No rest and no peace
In a house built of lies
April awakens
She opens her eyes

APRIL

I was finishing my daily household chores,
my parents with the cattle, as they are every morning.
I had finished the tidying and was sweeping the floor
when suddenly without reason, without any warning,
seven acorns dropped from a corner of the ceiling.
I was quickly overcome with the overwhelming feeling
that something was concealed in the place from which
    they'd dropped.
Seven acorns. It was as if time had stopped,
as if the dream had bled into my life.
I looked up to see the thatch had been disturbed,
and then, my curiosity and my suspicion
    both uncurbed,
I cut loose the thatch with my father's hunting knife.
  Between the oaken joists, I found a wooden box.
  In it, neatly folded, lay seven young men's smocks.

AND the dough it breathes
And the saw it swoons
And the cup and the plate
And the knife and the spoon
Huddle together
And sing to the moon
Truth drops
From the ceiling
Sometimes too late
But never too soon

JANE

Should I have thrown them away? Burned
them? Or buried them? Should I have spurned
forever my own sons? I could not.
To know their smocks were near me brought
back their memory, untied the knot
of my grief, comforted my heartache,
quenched a dreadful thirst I could not slake.
Those seven shirts are all that remains.
Destroying them erases, profanes,
the truth that *my* blood runs in their veins.
She came to me and I told it all—
every detail that I could recall,
the abhorrent and horrendous sight
of seven ravens taking flight,
how this cursed day was her birthright,
how when at last the birds retreated,
she sprang to life and death was cheated.
I cannot say what will happen next:
Truth has unforeseeable effects.

JACK

It's finally arrived, the dreadful day.
Let me alone. I've nothing to say.

APRIL

All of these years they have deceived me.
All of these years lying.
The ones who raised and conceived
me insist that they were only trying
to shield me. But shield me from what?
I want to believe them, but
I know too well they were protecting
themselves, hiding from the link connecting
my birth to my brothers' vanishing that day.
It wasn't me, but *truth* they could not face.
My brothers. Their sons. Gone with no trace.
But where there's a will, there is always a way.
   I can't say how or why, but I know it is my destiny
   to undo the raven spell and restore our
      broken family.

AND the sun shuts its eyes
And swallows the light
And April arises
In the blindness of night
And the cottage walls crack
And her small bag is packed
And the harp says *Take me*
And April is free
Away from her mother
Away from her father
Away from everything
Knowing her name
Away from the chores
The mop and the broom
She steps into darkness
Disappears in the gloom

JOURNEY

ANd the road is a villain
And the road is a friend
And the road is a story
No beginning no end
And the road is a question
And the road is an answer
And the road will transform you
A sly necromancer
And the road is a melody
And the road is a howl
And the road is a paradox
A grin and a scowl
And the road will not tell
Where it's been where it leads
And the road is alive
It sings and it bleeds

Who takes to the road
Can never return
For the road is a fire
All pilgrims will burn

APRIL

Is it days? Or months? Or years? Or weeks
that I have traveled this coarse and rugged
    thoroughfare?
Crossing cloud-topped mountains, chancing
    swollen creeks,
I've learned that time can be immeasurable as air.
There are moments I forget what I'm searching for,
and the only point is walking—walking, nothing more.
I tell myself momentum is its own reward
and that it's unimportant what I'm moving toward.
But I know it's only weariness that's speaking,
idle thoughts to guard against the pitfall of despair
when discouragement and solitude seem more than
    I can bear.
I know exactly what I'm seeking—
    my seven brothers, transformed, cast out, and lost.
    And I will find them. But I wonder at what cost.

HER journey continues
She walks ever on
Dusk after dusk
Dawn after dawn
She sleeps in the hay mounds
She eats what she finds
The road is a serpent
It twists and unwinds
She meets fellow travelers
The migrating throng
Each one is a question
A riddle a song
The scofflaw the sheriff
The pimp and the whore
The lover the hater
The tinker and more
The wounded crusader
The healthy the lame
Where are my brothers
Each answer's the same
Your brothers have vanished

They live in the trees
Gone in the dream-space
Like all memories

Our beaks pierce the clouds
Our talons are skewers
We scream in our sorrow
Each day is a misery
Each night is a torment
Cruel memory haunts us
Our heartbeats and marrow
Are phantoms that taunt us
Each tongue a defector
Betraying the songs
We once harmonized
Familiars of witches
We sully the skies

ROBYN

My brothers' pain is sharper, hotter, greater
    than my own. Back then, when I was still
a boy, every muscle, every vein,
    every heavy bone felt wrong. Every tree,
every stone, every table, every chair,
    even the very air I breathed, whispered,
You don't belong. My brothers yearn to be
    the way they were before. What I have come
to love they disparage and deplore. They
    miss their glory days and cry out for what
they've lost. But the sympathetic sun or
    winter's tender frost on my unclothed and
feathered back bring in turn a comfort and
    a thrill. I love my shining blackness, my
feathered legs, my bill, and especially
    my wings, like strong and steady oars, dipping
in the ocean of the wide and boundless
    sky. When I fly above the earth, from
my vantage in the consecrated blue,
    it helps me understand that everything
depends upon a changing point of view.

The house that seems so large below appears
so small above. Could this be true, I ask
myself, with all we hate and love?

ΛND the fields dream of rain
In their untroubled beds
And the boulders awake
And the grass lifts its head
And the bashful trees blush
And the streams and the hills
And the moss and the brush
Each sing a hymn
To each root and each trunk
And each leaf and each limb
And the vines and the saplings
Take in the bright air
And the pond shouts its name
And the mud drops its shame
And the nettles rejoice
And the pebble that's never
Been known finds its voice

APRIL

Every traveler I meet is a story
of anguish and joy, rancor and grace,
as if each soul is a repertory
of heartbreak and redemption. On each face
I see imprinted the indelible design
of a life's topography. Will that be true of mine
when I conclude what I've set out to do?
I think it must be so. For I've become a story too.
With each stony hill I climb, with every twist and bend
through sweeping unnamed forests, menacing
    and dense,
I leave behind my former self. My childish innocence
is fading, coming to its end.
    Perhaps my brothers' story is not so strange.
    Of only one thing am I certain: Life is change.

AND on the road
A withered crone
Pale of flesh
And frail of bone
Ignored by all
She sits alone
Underfed
Thin as a ghost
She is invisible to most
She looks each traveler
In the eye
They look away
They pass her by
Afraid her future
Is their own
Afraid of what
Her face has shown
Afraid their lives
Will be impacted
Afraid that they
Will be distracted
From their longings
From their missions
From their dreams

From their ambitions
But there is one
Who puts aside
Her own desires
Her urgent needs
She kneels beside
The outcast one
In the dust and dirt
And weeds

APRIL

The beldam asks me for a crust of bread
so quietly, I barely hear her speak.
Her poverty fills me with a choking dread,
on the road alone, so frail, so old and weak.
I share my loaf. She eats, and while I wait
I ask myself, *Is this to be my fate?*
To wander lost for all eternity
until my strength has fled, deserted me?
But in a voice that seems to find its youth
she tells me of a king she says will know
where my brothers are, and oh,
it has the certain ring of truth.

    Help has arrived from the least expected,
      from the untouchable, the wretched and neglected.

THE CRONE

Beware, you busy ones who pass me by as if I were
nothing more than dust to be despised or, worse, to be
dismissed. But I am more than meets the eye. Your
smug and sanctimonious disgust keeps you from the
help you most need to enlist.

Though all I whisper in your ear is true, truth's not
always evident or just; sometimes it's brutal as a fist.
You scratch your head. You wonder what to do.

You have no choice. You must persist.

SHE walks through tight valleys
The valleys sink deeper
She climbs treeless mountains
The mountains grow steeper
The moors become colder
The woodlands grow older
Sleet pummels her face
Her neck and her shoulders
Her legs bruised and heavy
She crosses high bridges
Thick levees and dams
She sleeps with the cattle
The goats and the lambs
Thorns tear and scratch
And nettles they sting
No ease and no respite
On the path to the king
The wind in her face
Is hard as a stone
She has no one to guide her
But she's never alone

APRIL

No matter how far I have traveled,
at the close of every day,
though my courage has unraveled,
I take out my harp and play,
and for a brief time, I am restored
by its spirited arpeggios and pacifying chords.
This harp has been my sole companion
on high and rocky cliffs, through barren,
     desert canyons.
It is a loyal friend and a vital part of me,
as essential to my being as the beating of my heart.
In its strings, its overtones, its art,
I feel the powerful vibrations of my destiny.
  I have many days to travel before I see the king.
  But when I reach my destination, I'll play for him
    and sing.

The noise of these woods
Grates and unsettles
The howl of the wolf
The huff of the bear
There is no joy
No solace there
The banshee winds
In the suffering trees
Where is the comfort
To be found in these
Our own raucous croaking
And coughing and cawing
And clicking and choking
And rasping revoking
The soft memory
Of the sad lilting airs
Our mother once sang
Now displaced by the wildwood's
Strident harangue

ROBYN

What my brothers call brash clamor and harsh
   cacophony, I consider calming
music and sweetest harmony. The low
   and moving plainsong of the sacred streams,
the a cappella carol of the trees,
   the mockingbird's hijacked motifs and themes,
the lyric humming of the choral bees
   are to me the most melodic sounds. If
I should be compelled to make a choice, I
   would choose these untamed fugues, descants,
     and rounds
over any manmade instrument or
   strident human voice. But sometimes when I'm
winging through the clouds, I hear, not floating
   on the air but harshly piercing it, a
maid's high, impassioned singing. And
   clinging like a leech to this high, unwelcome
song is that same unlit suspicion—
   something's very, very wrong. Just as in
our nightly keep, I feel a deep and
   cataclysmic change is on the way. How is

it possible I know this? I cannot
    say. But I have learned at last to trust my
intuition. It might be tomorrow.
    It could be today. And there is nothing
I can do to prevent it or prepare.
    I have only one refuge: The steady
sky, the loving air. And so I spread my
    wings and fly, mile on unmapped
mile, and force myself to let the feeling
    go, if only for a while.

APRIL

I see them in a vision almost every night,
my mother in the garden, my father in the forest,
each standing in a dreamed and shadowed light,
both suffering silently, heartbroken and depressed.
They struggle through their day-to-day routine.
Not knowing where I am or where I've been
has caused their hearts to break. Fraught
with guilt, they regret how earnestly they taught
me to do always the right thing.
But it was only empty talk, a figure of speech.
Parents should be careful about what they teach;
no one can predict the trouble it might bring.
  I will always be their daughter, but I will never
    be the same.
  There is nothing to forgive. There is no one
    to blame.

JACK

With every step I miss my daughter.
She's in the air I breathe, the water
that I drink, the meat and bread I eat.
Nothing can be whole, nothing complete,
every day a meaningless repeat
of the sorry day that came before.
The future is but a bolted door
until the time I see her again.
What a tribulation this has been.
We should be a family of ten.
My wife, my sons, my daughter, and me.
A proper size for a family.
But it's only us, just us, just two.
If only I could go back, undo
the curse, begin again, start anew,
I'd work to be more understanding,
less critical and less demanding
of all my boys, including Robyn.
Let him walk the path untrodden.

JANE

How easy it is for him—regret;
how hard it is for me to forget.
Because of him, I have lost them all.
My children now? Anger and Gall.
I have tried so often to recall
our greener, younger, happier days.
But they are gone, lost in a rank maze
of resentment and acrimony.
I don't know what has happened to me.
I used to be so light and carefree.
But losing your children changes you.
Your life is suddenly turned askew.
There is no good reason to go on.
Every morning is gray; every dawn
screams: *Your children are gone.*
I know only, as long as I live,
I won't forget. I won't forgive.
Until all my children have returned,
he'll have to live with what he has earned.

SHE enters a desert
The hot wind is blowing
The ember sky glowing
The hungry sand flowing
Like rivers with banks
Neither constant nor firm
The serpents are singing
The scorpion's stinging
The vultures are winging
The insect and worm
Torment and hector
Mirages and specters
Deceive and confuse
But she perseveres
Through danger through tears
Despite her young years
She has refused
To surrender her quest
She longs to know what
The future might bring
And puts all her hope
In the all-knowing king

THE KING

The adders, lizards, and the roaches
are hissing that a girl approaches.
The maid must be in deep despair
to face this desert's burning air,
these howling winds, these shifting sands,
these desiccated shadowlands.
They say she seeks the disappeared,
brothers who were commandeered
by some unnatural wizardry,
an equalizing sorcery
that captured them, then set her free.
But does she know what I'm king of?
King of Kindness?
King of Love?
King of Hope?
King of Desire?
King of Judgment?
King of Fire?
King of Laughter?
King of Dance?
King of Lust?
Or Abstinence?

King of Peace?
King of War?
So many kings to bow before.
When she arrives and bends her knee,
to which of these kings shall it be?
Her coming here was bold but rash,
for I am only King of Ash,
desert where there once was sea,
the Monarch of Despondency.

APRIL

This landscape is foreboding, stark and bare,
its shrieking wind ferocious. How it stings!
I see no living creature anywhere.
But deserts, too, I know, must have their kings.
This barren land is where my way has led,
but I have faith in what might lie ahead.
The crone would not have sent me here
if I had anything to fear.
She said he knows the place my brothers dwell,
that hermitage impossible to find.
He is a king: I know he will be kind
when he hears the tale I have to tell.
    My legs are weak. My heart is beating fast.
    Injustice will be rectified at last.

THE KING

Once I had dreams. They shined like gold.
Once I was young. Now I am old.
Dreams transform from gold to lead.
Once they lived. Now they are dead.
I do know where her brothers dwell;
I know, yes, but will not tell.
When all is said, when all is done,
why give her hope when I have none?

ANd the snakes bite their tails
And the empty wind wails
And the moon turns her back
And the earth starts to crack
And the sun screams and burns
And the pines and the oaks
And the moss and the ferns
Far from the desert
Wither and die
While the wasp the mosquito
The pestilent fly
And the death-hungry vulture
Take to the sky

APRIL

I come to him a supplicant, pleading, kneeling,
but asking for so little.
What bitter disappointment makes him so unfeeling,
so weak, so cruel and brittle,
that he knows but will not share where to find
    my brothers?
He whispers it is childish to care about the suffering
    of others,
that all is only barren stone and sterile dust.
When I tell him he is wrong, as I know I must,
a fearful thing occurs that I do not understand:
The sky above me shakes, the earth beneath
    me rumbles,
and with a dreadful sigh he collapses, crumbles
into a lifeless, windblown pile of desert sand.
    I have never felt more frightened or alone.
    Why did I dare to trust that deceiving,
        ancient crone?

THE CRONE

I did not say the king would tell her what he knew.
Poor girl! Her memory deceives, but as so often with
the immature, she heard exactly what she wanted to,
and so to soothe herself she believes I lied to her.

But I know where her true path lies, if only she will
listen and believe. The choice is hers; the outcome is
unsure. Next time, she will find me in disguise.

Will she endure?

SHE walks through the seasons
The hot stone of summer
Its breath suffocates her
The oxblood of autumn
It curdles and stains
The phantoms of winter
They shriek and bedevil
The hornets of spring
They needle her pain
Where are her brothers
How long must she wander
What more must she suffer
What more must she give
Where are the boys
Whose cruel transformation
Whose truncated lives
Allowed her to live

Our feathers are pinpricks
Our wings aberrations
Our beaks angry thorns
Our language is death
Can nobody help us
Restore and redeem us
Let us dream human dreams
Let us breathe human breath

ROBYN

We *live* a dream, or so it seems to me,
and breathe the breath of rampant liberty.

APRIL

I have heard persistent rumors of a mighty queen,
a ruler of philosophers and fools.
They say her palace is of tourmaline
and her throne of idols' pearls and stolen jewels.
The monarch of all prescient winds that blow,
there is nothing she can't see or doesn't know.
Even now I'm headed toward that fearful place.
I'll humbly kneel before her. I'll boldly plead my case.
That so-called desert king of emptiness and pain—
could she be worse? I've seen how heartless men
      can be.
But what has that to do with me?
Let her show me her contempt, her scorn,
      and her disdain.
   I will not stop until my brothers' mystery is solved.
   The more that I am tested, the more I am resolved.

THE CRONE

That rumor—where did it originate? What set it floating
through the air to reach the young girl's waiting ear?
Was it accident? Or was it fate? It's a mysterious affair—
the things that come to us, the things we hear.

She thinks her choices are her own, unenlightened,
unaware of forces from another sphere, enigmatic and
unknown.

Invisible. But always near.

ΛND the air is a blade
And the girl is the stone
On which it is sharpened
Polished and honed
And snowflakes like pebbles
They sting as they pelt
And nothing will give
And nothing will melt
And the snow it is drifting
And the faithless ice shifting
And the world has gone white
And even the night
Cannot put on its mantle

APRIL

When, like today, the ice and snow are deep,
when the air is cruel and slaps and bites and stings,
when the forward way slows me to a creep,
I turn my mind to more congenial things
and think about my seven brothers.
Their father is my father, their mother, my mother,
so I wonder if they are at all like me.
And I think of Robyn especially.
They told me he was different from the rest.
But it was difficult to know their exact intent.
Sensitive—I think that's what they meant,
but there was so much they were unwilling to express.
  If true, his torment must be worse.
  Oh, what a happy day when I free him from
    the curse.

ROBYN

I know there must be things I miss about
    my former life, but if so, they are too
distant to recall. What I remember
    most? The days rife with anxiety, the
fear, all the confusion. What did I want?
    What was wrong with me? At the exclusion
of my own happiness, I ached for dull
    normality. I regret that I was
not more courageous then. But that was in
    the past. I will not be so timorous again.
As for now, of only one thing am I
    certain: When I'm soaring in the dazzled
morning light, or when evening drops her
    cobalt velvet curtain, there is no wrong;
there is only right. Each feather is a
    shining dusky mirror, reflecting all
there is in opalescent black. Look
    carefully! It could not be clearer:
The beauty of the world shines on my back.

AND nothing can live
And nothing can die
She is struggling through
The inside of an eye
Desolation before her
Blankness behind
An eye that's polluted
An eye that is blind
And just when despair
And surrender convene
She comes to the place
Of the boreal queen

THE QUEEN

My cunning winds, cold and conniving,
are telling me a girl's arriving.
Fair of form and fair of face,
she's journeyed to this northern place
to ask me for some help she needs.
She hopes that I will intercede
to break an unjust conjury.
What nerve! What rash audacity!
To find her way here, uninvited,
through this landscape, frigid, blighted—
cracking ice and blinding snow.

This is, I think, a girl to know.

Courageous, filled with confidence,
more than her share of impudence—
her coming here is proof of that.
To brave this daunting habitat
she must be strong, unstoppable,
tenacious, bright, formidable,
with inner fire, ferocity.

She is, in fact, a girl like me.
Oh, this will be her lucky day.
I'm searching for a protégé.

APRIL

Her palace is not tourmaline but gold,
with tall and pointed spires of platinum
and every priceless thing that loves the cold.
The hall sits like a lustrous diadem,
rising from a flat and treeless plain,
surrounded by a moat, completely drained
and tiled with images of beasts in abalone,
then filled to near the top with rare and
     precious stones—
rubies, emeralds, sapphires, jade,
carnelians, jaspers, peridots—
jumbled all together like discarded thoughts
that once were welcomed, then betrayed.
    I know I should feel wonder, but instead
    I quake at its frigidity. I'm filled with icy dread.

THE QUEEN

What does the girl have to fear?
There's nothing that will harm her here.
She is misguided, young, naïve.
I simply want to help relieve
her of her sentiment.
The feeling heart's a detriment
and sure to lead to bleak regret.
I will teach her to forget
her hapless brothers.
All that is past,
for nothing which is mortal lasts.
Far better to embrace the art
of loving that which has no heart—
silver, platinum, garnet, gold.
The love that they give back is cold,
but being so, it cannot burn.
It asks for nothing in return.
Always constant, always true,
lapis will be always blue.
No other colors 'neath its skin.
No treason hiding deep within.

Once there lived a handsome prince
who wooed a maid and soon convinced
her to concede him all:
her heart, her soul, her bed, her hall.
She did not know it was a game.
He left her with remorse and shame.
She trusted love and paid the price.
Her heart contracted, turned to ice,
and taught the maid what it had learned:
The love that's true is love that's spurned.

BIRDS drop from the trees
And the sap starts to freeze
And each leaf is a blade
And the deer in the shade
Cannot move cannot run
Cannot lift her head
And the fawn in her womb
Shudders once
And is dead

APRIL

With viper eyes, she tells me I must sever
all family ties, all connection,
now, completely and forever.
And if to this profane defection
I will bind myself and swear,
I will, in time, become her heir
and so receive as my reward
her frozen realm, her golden horde.
She shuts her eyes. She whispers, *Trust me.*
She is both angry and confused
when I shrink back, when I refuse
and tell her that such thoughts disgust me.
    I run and leave her there alone.
    When I look back, she turns to stone.

AND hope is a country
Whose shoreline recedes
And hope is a garden
Blooming with weeds
Hope is a journey
Into the night
No guiding star
No comforting light
And hope is a paradox
Cousin to dread
And hope is cool water
And hope is warm bread
Hope is a burden
Unwieldy its load
And hope is a stranger
She meets on the road

APRIL

It is impossible for me to know her age,
as if she is both old and young, plain and fair.
She says that she has found me to assuage
my pain. She blinks her eyes and tells me where
my brothers are. In a mountain made of glass,
there is a door through which I have to pass.
It is here, at end of every day,
she swears my seven brothers find their way.
She hands me a pocket made of silk,
which holds the key to the mountain's door.
There has never been such a key before,
carved from chicken bone, and white as whitest milk.
   She promises that all will be restored, the curse at
      last suspended,
   that my wandering is over, my trials finally ended.

THE CRONE

Old or young or fair or plain. Future, past, or present
tense. Eclipsed moon or shining sun. The everyday
or the arcane. Gold or myrrh or frankincense. I am all
of these, and none.

She has persisted and transcended all hardships and
impediments. Her journey now is nearly done.
Yes, all her trials soon will be ended—

all of them but one.

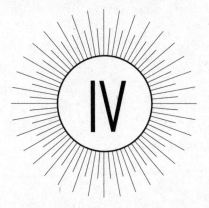

CHANGE

APRIL

Can it be real that it's coming to an end?
By tomorrow at the latest I'll arrive.
Thanks to that kind and unknown friend,
the adversities and hurdles that contrived
to hold me back are now behind me.
I'll have only my memories to remind me
of all the difficulties suffered through.
Now I have just one task left to do:
unlock the mountain's door
and free them from their misery.
The stranger said that when they see
that I have come, they'll instantly transform to the
     way they were before.
  I will love them all. I know that's true.
  But I'm sure it will be Robyn who I'll be closest to.

ROBYN

I have been thinking of the past and all
    I would do differently if it were
possible that I could. There was so much
    about myself I didn't know, so much
I misunderstood, like that day I saw
    the wakeful shadow standing near my un-
born sister's cradle, the forceful way it
    stared at me, demanding my attention.
How frightened I was then and how badly
    shaken. But my fear and apprehension
were almost comically mistaken. I
    was not in the grim presence of a low
and evil envoy from the land of the
    unliving. That opaque and moving shade
was the essence of a raven, giving
    me a gift, a glimpse of what was yet to
be. It had not come for the baby,
    but was there instead for me. How strange that
memory moves so freely through the
    corridors of time. That baby's but an
actor in a distant pantomime, and
    insignificant to me. The trees,

the streams, the hidden glades are now my
  family. I have no need for more, nor
do I pine for any other. My father is
  the steadfast sun, the watchful moon my
mother.

AND the road is a ribbon
Shining and straight
And the road is her guide
And her friend and her fate
And the road is a dove
Spreading its wings
And her hands are wild roses
When she plays on her harp
And she sings and she sings
She sings of the cottage
The axe and the hen
A mother and father
The shocking day when
Her brothers the Seven
Were cruelly exiled
And she sings of her journey
Each altering mile
And she sings of a king
Whose kingdom was Grief
And she sings of a queen
Whose only belief
Was in what she could own
And she sings of a stranger

And she sings of a crone
And she sings of a key
Fashioned from bone

What is that soothing melody
We hear
That human voice so loving
And so clear
Whose timbre and whose humble
Eloquence
Recall our cherished mother's
Resonance
How is it that this soulful air
Comes winging
To this drear and melancholy
Place
Why do those harp strings and
That singing
Alleviate our pain and
Our disgrace
What is that soothing melody
We hear
That human voice so loving
And so dear

ROBYN

What is that human melody I hear,
   unnatural in this wild and sacred place?
It fills me with that same recurring fear.
   Too soon I'll have to face the foreboding
premonition hiding deep within my
   chest. It warns me of a stranger with a
single-minded mission, and a dreadful
   change about to manifest. There is no
choice. I want to fly away, but to the
   mountain made of glass I must return by
end of day. I can't escape the feeling
   that all is fated. My present joy will
soon be devastated. But whatever
   lies ahead, this raven life has taught me
what it feels like to be free. There is no
   going back. I will not give that up so
easily.

AND the nightingale calls
In the fickle moon's light
And the mountain is shining
Translucent and bright
Inside are the brothers
Six and one more
April arrives
She stands at the door

SHE stands at the door
Not as she expected
She stands at the door
Crushed and dejected
She stands at the door
Alone and depleted
She stands at the door
Lost and defeated
She stands at the door
Weak of heart weak of knee
The door will not open

She has lost the bone key

THE CRONE

I've brought her here. I'll do no more. There is a choice
that she must make. The time has come; I'll disappear,
go back to what I was before, sleeping and awake.

My work for now is finally done. I leave her waiting
on the shore with everything at stake. Like all of us,
like everyone,

she stands at the door.

ΛPRIL

I've come so far and yet I've learned so little.
In many ways, I see I'm still a child.
My life remains a mystery, a riddle,
a ledger that must be ever reconciled.
The journey that brought me to this place
was nothing next to what I now must face.
The so-called key, that brittle chicken bone,
was nothing but a stand-in for my own.
From the handle of this heavy barricade,
someone, a loving friend or bitter foe—
the king? the queen? the crone? I'll never know—
has hung a keen and shining crystal blade.
  I understand: My *finger* is the key.
  My brothers? Or my hand? It's up to me.

ΛND she picks up the harp
Its frame and its strings
And her fingers are rain doves
And she sings and she sings
She sings of her journey
And all it has cost
And she sings of her hands
And what will be lost
And the trees drop their leaves
And the stones shed hard tears
And the wood turtle grieves
And the termite appears

She puts down the harp
She'll play it no more
And the knife it is sharp
And she opens the door

ΛND wings become arms
And talons are feet
And beaks drop to the floor
And the meeting is sweet

Our sister has saved us
From what we have been
The spell has been broken
We are whole
We are men

And there's blood where she stands
But what does it matter
The spell has been broken

The glass mountain shatters

BUT Robyn is silent
He too has transformed
His torso his legs
His head and his face
He has retained
All his lightness and grace
As if a great artist
Sculpted and molded
But in place of his arms
Black wings are now folded

ΛPRIL

What is this terrible mistake?
He trembles there in limbo like a ghost.
I must be dreaming. I cannot be awake:
Robyn, who I was sure to love most,
is caught between one world and another.
Robyn, my seventh brother,
was everything I sacrificed in vain?
Must I lose another finger? Maim myself again?
But he will not speak, will not say a word.
Our brothers' celebrations are raucous, loud, and shrill,
while he stands there so silently, unknowable, and still,
trapped in some uncharted place between humanity
    and bird.
  What have I done? How can this be?
  He turns his head away and will not look at me.

ROBYN

How can I look into my sister's eyes?
　　How can I show her what I feel? Should I
scream how her unasked-for good intentions
　　have taken me from everything I loved?
Shout that her misplaced intervention has
　　shoved me back into a world that I have
willingly forsaken? Should I tell her
　　she's to blame? There is no point. What I am
now? It has no name. I am not raven.
　　Nor am I man. Instead I am some other
thing. Some other thing again.

ΛND the strings of the harp
Tighten and snap
And the frame splits and cracks
And the sound box collapses
And the tuning pins rot
And nothing remains
But splinter and knot
And wings once carved
Into the harp's frame
Lift from the ruin
And burst into flame

EPILOGUE

APRIL

How quickly circumstances normalize.

Now home, my brothers take their place beside our
father. Each dawn, they arise as if all that has occurred
has been erased, while Robyn stays alone in a thatched
hut that our loving parents built for him. Just what he
feels, we do not know. He is aloof. But there are always
ravens on the roof.

My father said he wants to carve another harp for me,
one that can be played with my poor disfigured hand,
but I told him he must wait. I am not ready yet. I am
beset with a steady melancholy and cannot find the
spirit that music demands.

I think of what has come to pass and try to find some
time each day to spend alone. I dream often of the
mountain made of glass, the helpful stranger and the
crone, and am struck with the comforting idea that
they are always with me, always near. The same is
true for the king and queen, though that feeling is
more unsettling.

As for my finger, it sometimes gives me pain, the finger that is no longer there. I feel it strongly, throbbing in the air, pulsing like an unforgettable refrain.

If I knew now . . . would I do it all again? How can I know? I was a different person then.

ROBYN

How quickly circumstances normalize.
    My younger days and *now* are much the same.
The difference is I am not willing to
    disguise all that I am. And so the guilt,
the nagging doubt, the shame I felt, are now
    part of the past. No, I am *not* an outcast,
as I so wrongly thought before, but a
    preview of the possible, something new
and something more. I dream I am a house
    with endless rooms and endless doors.
Are you an angel? the curious
    inquire. I answer, *It's conceivable.*
To angelhood I happily aspire
    for such a life must be rare and beautiful.
So do not shake your worried heads and sigh.
    Yours is the earth . . .

But I possess the sky.

ΛND the trees they are singing
And the ravens are winging
And the world celebrates

And the forest awaits.

Λ NOTE ΛBOUT POETIC FORM

I love formal poetry, that is, poetry with a prescribed form. And I especially love it in the context of a novel in verse. Some might fear that the rules of each form will restrain the writer. But I have found the opposite to be true. In fact, the rules liberate, helping to shape and inform the book's various voices. When a character speaks always in haiku, for example, she tells us something about who she is, as distinct from, say, her counterpart who holds forth in long-winded ballads.

Below, you will find the forms I used in *The Seventh Raven*. To the purists among you, I apologize for the idiosyncrasies—some might call them blunders—by which I sometimes flout the rules. To the more forgiving, I am grateful for your spirit of generosity.

ROBYN

When human, Robyn speaks in the rondeau, a French form of fifteen lines in which the opening phrase of the first line repeats at lines nine and fifteen ("they called me Robyn" in his first poem). This repetition, plus the rhyming of just two words, constricts the form. This tightness seemed to parallel

Robyn's feelings as a young man. But when he is a raven, free of his human constraints, it seemed to me he needed to express himself in a form that was less binding. In early drafts, he spoke in a standard fourteen-line Shakespearean sonnet. While the sonnets worked well enough as sonnets, as Robyn's voice they were still too limiting. Not only that, but they gave him a kind of superior feeling. *Look at me*, he seemed to be saying. *I can speak in sonnets!* What to do? In the spirit of sustainability, I repurposed his poems. That is, I took the sonnets apart, used what I thought was working, discarded what wasn't, and added lines when fourteen weren't sufficient for what he wanted to say. Now he speaks—more or less—in ten-syllable lines, which sometimes are sonnet-like and sometimes aren't.

APRIL

Originally, there was a talking bear in the book. (Don't ask.) The bear is, of course, a symbol of Russia, so in those early days a Russian form seemed appropriate for April. I settled on the Onegin stanza, sometimes called the Pushkin sonnet because it was invented by the great Russian writer Alexander Pushkin. (Pushkin used this form in his own verse novel, *Eugene Onegin*.) The sonnet requires seven sets of rhyming words in each stanza. It also employs both masculine (stressed) and feminine (unstressed) rhymes. I confess that I did not adhere to this latter requirement. April's last poem consists of two stanzas (and a variation or two) of this form but with different formatting, a visual representation, I hope, of her own transformation and change. Sadly, that talking bear didn't make it into the final draft. But the sonnet stayed.

JACK/JANE

Robyn and April's parents speak in a Welsh form, Cyhydedd Naw Ban. (Don't ask.) Each line has nine syllables, plus or minus in my rendering. But the poet has some freedom when it comes to the rhyme pattern. In my version, the pattern is as follows: couplet, triplet, couplet, triplet, couplet, triplet, couplet, couplet. Because we often experience our parents as a single unit, I thought it right that Jack and Jane speak in the same form.

THE CRONE

Though it looks different on the page, the crone speaks in the form invented by Gerard Manley Hopkins in his famous and beautiful poem "Pied Beauty." I was happy to discover that the brief final line of the form works to intensify the crone's ambiguity.

KING/QUEEN

Both the king and queen speak in couplets.

NARRATIVE POEMS

These poems were inspired by "The House That Jack Built." Each line has two beats. To my ear, when read aloud, this lends a hypnotic effect suggesting another time, another place. In other words, *once upon a time.*

Once upon a time. Five syllables that have the power, perhaps more than any others, to transport us to our deepest selves, for fairy tales are not merely stories to entertain us. They are also intricate pictures of the human experience, generated in and by our ancestors and passed down to us through the ages. Tales, the *real* tales, are vessels that help us navigate the existential dilemmas that sooner or later we all must face. Passed on from generation to generation in cultures from Azerbaijan to Zimbabwe, they teach us how to live.

I have always loved the Grimms' lesser-known story "The Seven Ravens" and what it seems to say about masculine energies run amok, about the power of perseverance to transform and unite, about sacrifice. And above all, the powerful message that if we are to inherit the kingdom, we must enter the forest alone.

OTHER NOVELS IN VERSE
BY DAVID ELLIOTT

Bull

Voices: The Final Hours of Joan of Arc

ABOUT THE AUTHOR

David Elliott is a *New York Times* best-selling author whose recent works include *Bull* and *Voices,* both critically acclaimed novels in verse, with ten starred reviews between them. Born in Ohio, David has worked as a singer, a cucumber washer, and a Popsicle stick maker. Currently, he lives in New Hampshire with his wife and dog. Visit davidelliottbooks.com.